For Xia and a good dog, Baron—K.B.

To Stefano, the boy in my dream—N.C.

Text copyright © 2008 by Kate Bernheimer
Illustrations copyright © 2008 by Nicoletta Ceccoli
All rights reserved.
Published in the United States by Schwartz & Wade Books, an imprint of
Random House Children's Books,
a division of Random House, Inc., New York.

Schwartz & Wade Books and colophon are trademarks of Random House, Inc.

www.randomhouse.com/kids

Educators and librarians, for a variety of teaching tools,
visit us at www.randomhouse.com/teachers

Library of Congress Cataloging-in-Publication Data
Bernheimer, Kate.
The girl in the castle inside the museum / Kate Bernheimer; illustrated
by Nicoletta Ceccoli. — 1st ed.
p. cm.
Summary: Children come to visit a little girl who lives all alone inside
a castle, which is housed inside of a museum.
ISBN 978-0-375-83606-0 (trade) — ISBN 978-0-375-93606-7 (lib. bdg.)
[1. Castles—Fiction. 2. Museums—Fiction.] I. Ceccoli, Nicoletta, ill.
II. Title.    PZ7.45566Gi 2008 [E]—dc22
2006101854

The text of this book is set in Belen.
The illustrations are rendered in acrylic paint,
clay models, photography, and digital media.
Book design by Rachael Cole

PRINTED IN CHINA
10 9 8 7 6 5 4 3 2 1
First Edition

# The girl in the Castle inside the Museum

written by Kate Bernheimer

pictures by Nicoletta Ceccoli

schwartz & wade books · new york

$O$nce upon a time, there
was a girl who lived in a castle.

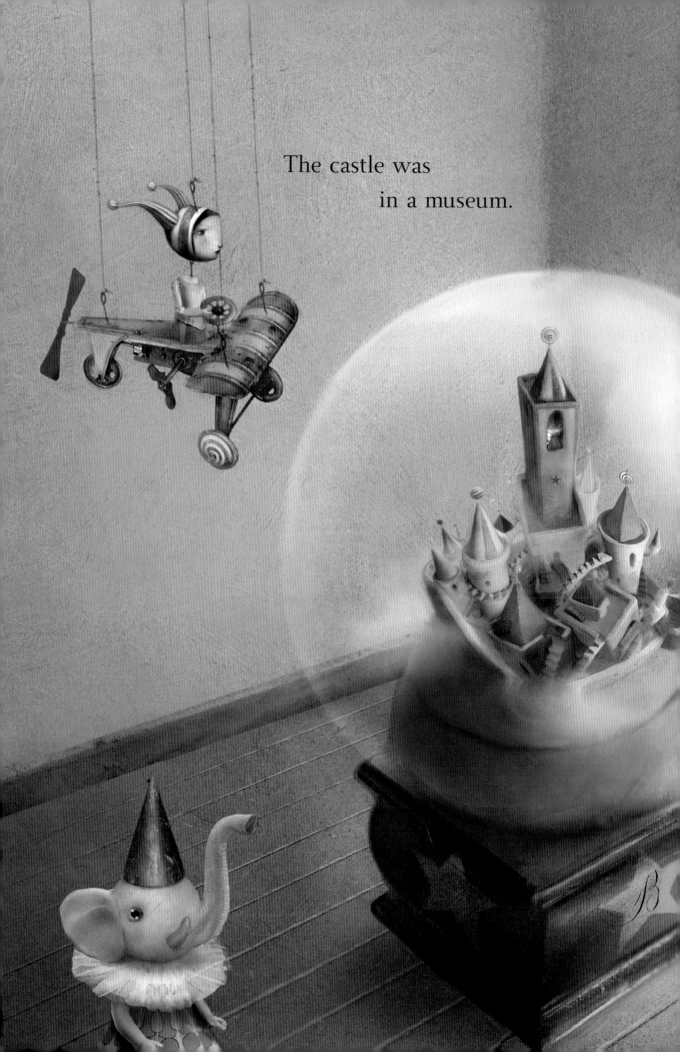

The castle was
in a museum.

When children came to the museum,
they pressed as close as they could to the
glass globe in which the castle quietly sat.

For they had heard if they looked hard enough,
they could see the girl who lived inside,

the girl in the castle inside the museum.

There, through that window, right there.

Do you see her?

It's been said
she's lived there
forever.

Sometimes the girl is lonely when the children go home.

But oh, it is beautiful!
There are moats and turrets
and bright shining lamps.
There are dark winding streets
that gleam in the rain.

The castle is full of
music and grace.

There is even a tower, the girl's favorite place.
Inside that tower she sits.
And inside that tower, at night she dreams.
What does she dream of, the girl in the castle
inside the museum?

"Once upon a time," her dream begins,
"a boy lived in a house inside the deep woods.

One day he walked down a path of toadstools
till he came to the museum and visited me."

"Once upon a time," she dreams again,
"a girl lived in a town where the sun hardly shone.

One day she walked down a road lined with flowers

till she came to the
museum and visited me."

Sometimes the girl
in the castle
even dreams about you.

The girl can be lonely
when she wakes up.

But look!
She has
an idea.

She wants a picture of you for the wall—
to hang in the tower alongside her bed.
Then she won't have to miss you at all.

*Dear Friend,*
*Please leave a picture*
*of yourself here for me.*

Now in her room and in her dreams,

inside the castle inside the museum,

inside this book you hold in your hands,

you keep her company in a magical world.

Do you see her? She sees you.